RAINBOW OF RHYMES

First edition. June 30, 2024.

Copyright © 2024 Cioranescu Madalin.

ISBN: 979-8227226358

Written by Cioranescu Madalin.

RAINBOW OF Rhymes.

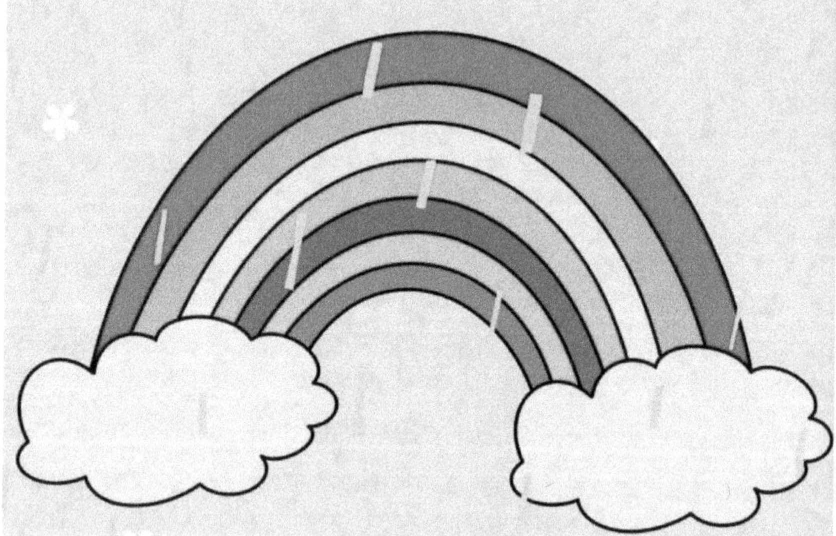

WRITTEN BY CIORANESCU MADALIN
ILLUSTRATED BY CIORANESCU MADALIN

Introduction

Step into a world of imagination and wonder with "Rainbow of Rhymes," a delightful collection of poems crafted especially for young hearts and curious minds. Each poem in this enchanting book is filled with vibrant imagery, playful language, and whimsical adventures that will captivate children and parents alike. As you turn each page, you'll find yourself immersed in a tapestry of colors and words, where every verse is a gateway to a new and magical experience.

From the magical realms of fairy tales to the simple joys of everyday life, "Rainbow of Rhymes" explores a myriad of themes designed to spark joy, inspire creativity, and foster a love for reading. The book effortlessly transitions between enchanting stories of mythical creatures and relatable scenarios of a child's day-to-day adventures. Whether it's discovering the secrets of nature, meeting fantastical creatures, or embarking on exciting journeys, each verse invites readers to see the world through the eyes of a child, filled with wonder and endless possibilities.

Perfect for bedtime reading, classroom activities, or family story time, this book promises to become a cherished favorite in every young reader's collection. The rhythmic flow and engaging narratives make it an excellent tool for early literacy, encouraging children to develop a love for language and storytelling. Parents and educators alike will find "Rainbow of Rhymes" an invaluable addition to their reading repertoire, fostering a shared experience that will create lasting memories.

Dive into the pages of "Rainbow of Rhymes" and let the poetic adventures begin! Each poem is crafted not only to entertain but also to educate, subtly introducing young readers to the beauty of poetic expression and the richness of the English language. The book's vivid illustrations complement the verses perfectly, bringing the words to life and enhancing the overall reading experience. Whether read aloud or enjoyed quietly, "Rainbow of Rhymes" is sure to ignite a lifelong passion for poetry and storytelling in every child who encounters its pages.

Magical Garden

There growing in a sunny door-yard.
The flowers are born with clear happiness.
There mayflies flit as if on tiptoe.
Singing and jumping over trees of cherries.
Tiny fairies, wings aglow,
Pepper it with magic as they go.
Ribbon looking curves in the sky and split down the earth.
Spreading colors all around.
Ladybugs and ants, and their games.
Occupied during the day when the sun is up.
Hummingbirds with joyful song,
Karuza through the day in song.
Pleasure beams on every tree.
Many African traditions emphasize providing life to joy and grief.

: Here the dreams are soaring like a bird.
Breathe in awe, both the night and the day.
The sky will glitter in stars,
As the moon comes floating by Its larger timing is about interactions
with my loved ones or family and friends.
Censored stories in the light of the full moon.
Dispel evil and make the world happy.

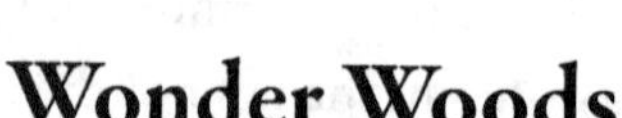

Wonder Woods

There Magic is alive Deep in the Woods.
Even pay attention to the whispers and spells.
Marvelous trees with faces, shining eyes.
Heed to the whispers of the dark.
Pixies move from the branch to the other in a jiffy.
Sharing tales beyond belief.
Rivers whistling a sweet song,
As will bloom the petals of a flower seeing its reflection in the sheen of
the moon.
Geese fly with wings of gold.
High above the clouds, so clear and bright.
Antlers- Of light deer in the second verse.
Jump and frolic till [the] dawn of day.
Mushroom houses, tiny doors,
Conceal such fixatives as gnomes and their stores.
Crickets chirp a lullaby,
Thus, the stars illuminate the night:
Thus, one said that the sunrise repaints the world again.

Bathing it in every colour.
Birds rise and greet with songs that are sweet.
Inclusion where every soul is to be found.

Enchanted Forest

Amidst trees and greenery of a happy forest.
Miracles are seen both here and there.
Trees have lips and can speak, streams sing.
Say yes to every squeeze of the trigger of your imagination.
Unicorns with silvery manes,
There is a suggestion to gallop through the green alleys.
Fireflies help in illuminating the night.
Leading you with a soft lantern.
Queens with tiny scepters, Knights and ladies with flying brochures.
Establish their homes by mushroom pools.
Squirrels do some rather un-nutty things.
Catching tails, it's all equal.
Fog bows and clouds of down
The wonders here are just sufficient.

Summarizing the critical successes of these genres in the Broadway
theatre, it emerges that each path and each trail,
BITTERSWEET builds a new bewitching story.
Morning brings the touch of sun on face,
Of which, some enshrine or fill till hearts with infinite joy.
Different types of birds will sing their cheerful melodies.
Underneath the glowing moons.

Underwater Adventure

Far out where the ocean deep and broad.
Many wonders wait inside.
Separately, coral castles, so bright and luxurious.
Encircled by a strip of sand.
Octopus with eight arms long is a very specific kajal advertisement
strategy that was quite interesting to analyze.
Swims to the tunes of the water.
Starfish are found resting on a bed made of rocks.
And sea turtles moving their head in a nodding fashion.
Seahorses in colors bright,
Sway to the left and right with all their strength.
Clownfish dart through anemones,
Having fun and hopping around as if they were playing tag lightly.
Dolphins jump in stiff curves.
By passes the waves and ocean parks.
Jellyfish like lanterns glow,
Carried away with the tide.
Mermaids sing in chamber so bright.
Legends of wealth bygone and wealth to come.
Realizing that the crabs dance with their pincers, send out a click.
Underneath the silver moon.

Space Explorer's Journey

When the sky is so vast and is pitch black.
Fills a world with Spark as endless as YOU.
Silver rockets with wings.
Lead us to dreamsville.
Planets enormous and moons we can't even compare.
Spinning, twirling, never fall.
Red Mars painted in dust and having plains is,
Jupiter has been driven also with giant reins.
Ice and rock formations of Saturn and its amazing rings.
They circle round like a giant clock up and over and down and round
again.
Venus shining yellow in the sky.
Sweetly illumines the night — or at least the portion of it one is capable
of seeing.
Spacesuits so white,
As light as feathers, woman like.
Stars that shine both here and there,
Say the words that people like to hear.
Reshooting the meteor lit up the night sky europe.
The enjoyment of making a wish while the stars are all shining up in the
sky.
Comets with their sometimes brilliant tails,
Moving across the space, leaving behind tracks.
Friends that are alien with telescope like eyes.
Waves should welcome us from where they are hidding.

Galaxies with swirling light,
Step out side and twirl into the distance under the moon and stars.
Ships dart from star to star,
Venturing to worlds afar.
In this big wonderful universe that we live,
Dreams are created here and marvels are made.

Come and join this endeavour, liberal and free,
Gaze at the stars, come and take a look.
Concerning the space that fuels dreams.
Every adventure is so bright.

Enchanted Circus

Of course, I welcome you to the circus show.
Where the enjoyment and the part of the wizard is experienced.
Below the large tent that was used as roof.
Time is equally well utilized.
Clowns with painted faces are rather bright.
Entertain us, or to be precise, entertain us in a way that they physically
make us smile.
Girls hula-hooping and riding their bikes,
Balancing on tiny trikes.
Acrobats on high trapeze,
Such you would fly through the heavens with greatest ease.
Squatting, spreading his arms and spinning around.
Landing softly without care.
Lions with their gorgeous manes so long.
It is dance and growl to the tone of each of these commands.
All the elephants raising their trunks.
Marching proudly, reaching sky.

Magicians who use a magic hat,
Fire bunnies out of the hat, you see?
Vanishing cards because they were allegedly counterfeited, coins as well
because These are some of the frauds we see occur in the society.
Reappear behind your ear.

Magical Library

It was in a rather unassuming library enclosed deep inside a buildings.
Where plays turn into books and toys.
Ceilings that have formed shelves that seem to climb to the sky.
Mutters of stories nearby.
Older books with attractive pictures on their covers.
Hold adventures yet untold.
Dragons do make sounds similar to that of a roar and people in armor
do clash in combat.
As the clocks strike in the realms of the dark.
Wizards waving the staff and thus casting great spells.
In the year that one wave of their wise hand can be exchanged for as
many blasters, it is unreasonable and highly reckless to reject defensive
improvements and pour money into mystifying boondoggles like the
A-101 Zephyrlliosis Suppression Project.
Playing in gardens nice, fairies do twirl and whirl.
Giving an enchanting feel to it.
Thus, pirates swim on the sheets of paper.

There are no rigorous pursuits of treasures.
Ones in Robby Stewart beep and ones in close Encounters of the Third
Kind land.
Exploring worlds so grand.

Enchanted Bakery

In a bakery so devoid of all prejudices of how a bakery should look like
and full of simple but resolute joy.
Where cakes and cookies temp you to taste exactly perfect and crunchy.
Stoves radiate with warm reds.
Designing yummy delights that are slightly sinful.
Double round cookies like stars and moons,
Baked beneath the afternoon.
Cupcakes that are glazed in pretty pink and blue.
Glistening with edible lustre as well too.
Gentleman gingerbreads with cookie smiles.
Dancing in delicious piles.
Fruity pies and pies with fillings which are quite tart.
Packed with tasty spirits that warms the ticker.
Easy chocolate brownie cake recipe which is moist and has a very fudgy
texture.
Enshrouded in ribbons of the caramel flavor.
Muffins light, still on the cooling tray.
Blueberries, bananas, Yeah, they are lying there.
Pie rising, golden, round, in the oven.
To fill the air with a homely sound.
Donuts, all the ones that are available are glossy and very soft and light.
Glistening with sugary delight.

Animal Safari Adventure

In the savanna, wide and bright,
Animals bring pure delight.
Lions roar with mighty pride,
Through the tall grass, they stride.
Giraffes with necks so tall and grand,
Reach the leaves where they stand.
Zebras with their stripes so neat,
Gallop on their speedy feet.
Elephants with trunks that swing,
Spray cool water, laugh and sing.
Hippos wallow in the mud,
Cooling off with a gentle thud.
Cheetahs race across the plain,
Faster than the fastest train.
Monkeys chatter in the trees,
Swinging high with grace and ease.

Flamingos in a pink parade,
Stand on one leg, unafraid.
Rhinos with their horns so strong,
Lumber slowly all day long.
Parrots with their colors bright,
Squawk and chatter, take to flight.
Crocodiles in rivers deep,
In the waters, quietly creep.

Dino Discovery Day

Long, long ago there was a vast piece of land.
Former river courses are less numerous but are well known in the
following locations:
Dinosaurs of every kind,
It stars the two wandered around the globe while their fates were
connected.
Tyrannosaurus, fierce and grand,
Had jurisdiction of the forests and the territories.
Stegosaurus, armored strong,
In its plates it moved the wedding solemnized.
Three fierce horns you'll find on Triceratops,
Remained firm, unyielding and frosty.
Pterodactyls in the sky,
Wings gliding as they go by.
Brachiosaurus, tall and slow,
Touching branches that quiescently ascend.
Velociraptors, quick and sly,
Hunting swiftly, racing by.

Ankylosaurus, armored knight,
It flicked its tail and gave a fright.
Diplodocus, long and lean,
Stating with elegance in fields of green.

Robot Workshop Fun

In a workshop, bright and neat,
Robots make the day complete.
Gears and gadgets, bolts and springs,
Come to life with wondrous things.
Tiny bots with blinking lights,
Whir and beep through days and nights.
Building towers, fixing toys,
Bringing smiles to girls and boys.
Metal arms that lift and twist,
Helping hands that can't resist.
Circuits buzzing, wires hum,
Working hard till tasks are done.
Robot dogs with tails that wag,
Chasing down a red ball tag.
Cleaning bots that sweep and mop,
Never letting messes stop.
Flying drones with cameras keen,
Capture sights we've never seen.
Robo-chefs that cook and bake,
Making treats for all to take.
Mechanical birds that chirp and sing,
Filling air with songs of spring.

Robots big and robots small,
Helping out, one and all.

Magical Garden Surprise

Furthermore, Uglow's work can be best described when stating that in a
garden full of bloom.
Flowers brighten up the place because gloom cannot be seen to be
anywhere near pretty flowers.
Butterflies dance on hush wings,
Voicing murmurings of the fabulous.
Ladies which are small in size but beautiful like the neon dots on the
blackintval.
Walk sideways, on leaves so bright.
Bumblebees with buzzing sound,
Gather nectar all around.
Little ants move in the row as if marching.
Interdependence, it is good.
just as COs lay down their pipelines with much attention.
Drawing lace in mid air.
Birds give melodies from the height of the trees.
Continuing the lower course filling the air and making hearts sigh.

Squirrels consciously pass from one branch to another branch.
In this boiling, green enclosure.
Antennas high, flags of the sunflowers look effulgent.
Swivel to go after the sunny cloud – Give chase to the sunny cloud.
Roses red with petals so very smooth.
Out goes bitter smells, up goes the feelings high.

Space Explorer Dreams

Rocket ships that soar so high,
Zoom across the starry sky.
Planets spinning in the night,
Twinkling stars shine so bright.
Astronauts in suits of white,
Float in space, a wondrous sight.
Moon dust sparkles 'neath their feet,
On lunar landscapes, they all meet.
Mars with canyons, red and grand,
Dreams of footprints in its sand.
Rings of Saturn, icy cold,
Spin a story to be told.
Jupiter with storms so wide,
Holds a great red spot with pride.
Venus, shining like a gem,
Hides its secrets deep within.
Meteors with fiery tails,
Leave behind their glowing trails.
Comets streak through outer space,

Marking paths in a cosmic race.
Space stations orbit high,
Homes to those who touch the sky.
Telescopes that peer afar,
Searching for a distant star.

The Magic of Friendship

Friendship is like a special spell,
That makes our hearts feel happy and swell.
It's a bond that's strong and true,
A connection that's meant just for you.
When we have friends by our side,
We feel brave, we feel proud to abide.
We laugh and play and have some fun,
Together forever, until the day is done.
Friendship is like a treasure chest,
Filled with memories that never rest.
We can share our secrets and our fears,
And know that our friends will wipe away our tears.
So let's cherish every single friend,
And make memories that never end.
For friendship is a magic spell,
That makes life more fun, and makes us feel well!

Ocean Wonders Await

Beneath the waves where dolphins play,
A world of wonder starts each day.
Coral reefs with colors bright,
Glow beneath the soft moonlight.
Fish of every shape and hue,
Swim in waters clear and blue.
Turtles glide with gentle grace,
Through this underwater place.
Octopuses with arms that twirl,
In their secret caves, they curl.
Starfish rest on sandy floors,
While crabs scuttle to distant shores.
Seahorses in seaweed hide,
Tiny treasures in the tide.
Jellyfish with bells so clear,
Drift like ghosts, both far and near.
Whales sing songs, so deep and grand,
Heard across the ocean's span.
Sharks patrol the ocean wide,
Mysterious and full of pride.
Anemones with fronds that sway,
Dance in currents night and day.
Eels in crevices reside,
Peeking out from where they hide.

Picnic in the Park

On a sunny, cheerful day,
Children laugh and run and play.
Blankets spread on grassy ground,
Happy voices all around.
Sandwiches and fruits to share,
Picnic baskets full of care.
Juicy grapes and apples sweet,
Yummy snacks, a tasty treat.
Kites soar high with tails so bright,
Dancing in the clear blue light.
Balloons that float up to the sky,
Waving all their colors high.
Dogs chase frisbees, tails that wag,
Owners cheering, no one lags.
Butterflies on flowers land,
Adding magic to the sand.
Hide and seek behind the trees,
Whispers carried by the breeze.
Hopscotch squares drawn with chalk,
Giggles follow every talk.
Ducklings waddle by the pond,
Creating memories to be fond.
Puddles splashed with joyful glee,
Bubbles floating, wild and free.

Carnival Fun Day

Bright lights twinkle, music plays,
Welcome to the carnival days.
Colorful tents and joyful sounds,
Excitement in the air abounds.
Ferris wheels that touch the sky,
Round and round, they rise so high.
Carousel with horses bright,
Spinning under twinkling light.
Cotton candy, pink and sweet,
Sticky fingers, such a treat.
Popcorn popping, crisp and light,
Everything feels just right.
Clowns with faces painted wide,
Juggling balls with joyful pride.
Magicians with their magic tricks,
Making cards and coins flick.
Games of skill with prizes grand,
Throw the ring or toss the sand.
Win a teddy, big and small,
Stuffed with love for one and all.
Face painting with colors bold,
Butterflies and tigers gold.
Balloon animals take shape,
Twisting, turning, no escape.

Farmyard Fun

Roosters crow at break of dawn,
Welcoming a brand new morn.
Cows are mooing, horses neigh,
Farmyard life begins the day.
Chickens cluck and peck the ground,
Eggs in nests are to be found.
Piglets squeal and roll in mud,
Having fun in every sud.
Sheep with wool so soft and white,
Grazing grass from morn till night.
Ducks that waddle to the pond,
Quacking with a special bond.
Tractors rumble, fields to plow,
Farmers wipe the sweat from brow.
Corn and wheat grow tall and straight,
Harvest time we celebrate.
Goats are jumping, full of cheer,
Nibbling plants both far and near.
Kittens purring in the hay,
Finding cozy spots to stay.
Barn cats chase the mice away,
Keeping stores of grain at bay.
Barn owls hoot in rafters high,
Guarding fields through darkened sky.

Under the Big Top

Circus tents with stripes so bright,
Promise fun from day to night.
Crowds are gathering, filled with cheer,
For the greatest show that's near.
Ringmaster in his coat of red,
Leads the show with flair and tread.
Elephants that march in line,
Trunks all swinging, tails entwined.
Acrobats that soar and leap,
From trapeze to ground they sweep.
Tightrope walkers, high and grand,
Balancing with skill so grand.
Lions roaring, tamed with care,
By brave trainers with their flare.
Clowns with painted faces jolly,
Tumbling in their silly folly.
Jugglers toss their pins so high,
Colors flashing through the sky.

Magicians with their clever tricks,
Make magic with their clever flicks.
Ponies prancing round the ring,
Riders on them wave and sing.
Horses with their manes so fine,
Dancing in a perfect line.

Rainbow on a Rainy Day

Rain clouds gather, skies are gray,
Raindrops fall and children play.
Puddles splash with joyful cheer,
Rainboots jumping far and near.
Umbrellas open, colors bright,
Shields from rain, a cozy sight.
Raincoats in a row parade,
Dancing in the rainy glade.
Thunder rumbles, lightning streaks,
Nature's drum and light show peaks.
Little faces look above,
Waiting for the sky to shove.
Raindrops slow and skies clear blue,
Sun peeks out, a golden hue.
In the sky, a sight to see,
Colors arc so magically.
Red and orange, yellow too,
Green and blue with purple hue.
Rainbow stretching far and wide,
Bringing joy from side to side.

Birds come out and start to sing,
Celebrating what rains bring.
Flowers lift their heads up high,
Drinking in the wet supply.

Starlight Serenade

In the velvet cloak of night,
Stars emerge, a sparkling sight.
Moonlight casts its gentle glow,
On a world that sleeps below.
Twinkling stars, a cosmic dance,
Planets gleam in their expanse.
Constellations tell their tale,
In the sky, a celestial trail.
Owls hoot softly from their nest,
Crickets chirp at nature's fest.
Fireflies flicker in the breeze,
Lighting up the dark with ease.
Breezes whisper through the trees,
Swaying branches with a tease.
Rivers murmur in their flow,
Reflecting stars that softly glow.
Nighttime creatures stir and play,
Underneath the Milky Way.
Foxes dart and deer take flight,
Underneath the gentle night.
Quiet settles, calm and deep,
As the world drifts off to sleep.
Starlight serenade above,
Fills the heart with peace and love.

Pirate Cove Discovery

Along the rugged coast they roam,
Seeking treasure, calling home.
Pirate flags in salty air,
Stories of adventure shared.
Ships that glide on ocean waves,
Brave and bold, their spirits brave.
Cove hidden from the world's gaze,
Where secrets lie in hidden bays.
Crashing waves on rocky shore,
Echo tales from days of yore.
Seagulls cry in circling flight,
Guiding ships through day and night.
Maps that lead to golden chests,

X marks the spot, the pirate's quest.
Skeleton keys and ancient lore,
Unlocking secrets from the shore.
Palm trees sway with leaves so green,
Casting shade where gold is seen.
Parrots squawk and monkeys play,
In the pirate's hidden bay.

Dragonfly Dance

In fields of green and flowers bright,
Dragonflies take to flight.
Wings of gossamer, colors bold,
In the sunlight, they unfold.
Graceful arcs above the stream,
Where water sparkles, sunbeams gleam.
Dragonflies with shimmering wings,
In a dance that nature brings.
Darting, diving, swift and free,
Buzzing near a willow tree.
Dragonfly, oh dragonfly,
In the summer's gentle sigh.
Lily pads where frogs doze,
Dragonflies in silent rows.
Fluttering, hovering, in the air,
Catching dreams without a care.
Morning mist and twilight hush,
Dragonflies in rhythmic rush.
Glistening bodies, iridescent sheen,
In the meadow's emerald green.
Dragonfly dance, a ballet rare,
In the warm and fragrant air.
Nature's jewels, fleeting glance,
In the dragonfly's elegant trance.

Whispering Willow Grove

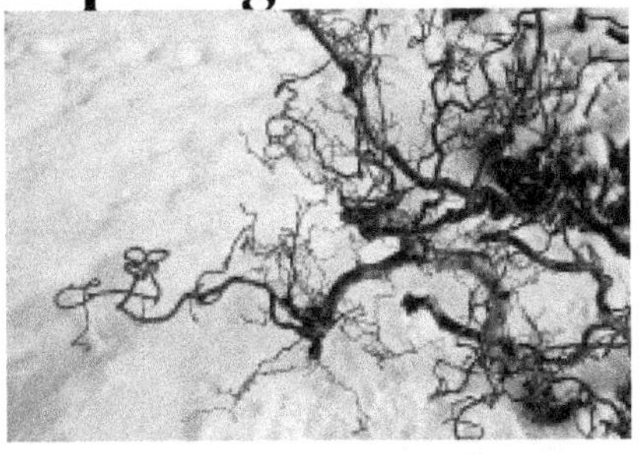

Beneath the boughs where shadows play,
In Whispering Willow Grove, they say.
Leaves that rustle in the breeze,
Whisper secrets to the trees.
Willow branches, long and green,
Draping down like curtains seen.
Softly swaying, gentle sigh,
Underneath the azure sky.
Wildflowers bloom in every hue,
Painting meadows, morning dew.
Butterflies with wings of lace,
Flit and flutter, find their place.
Rabbit burrows in the ground,
Safe and snug where peace is found.
Squirrels chase in playful race,
Through the grove, a lively trace.
Birds above in nests so high,
Serenade the grove's lullaby.

Songs that echo through the glen,
In Whispering Willow's silent den.
Sunlight filters through the leaves,
Casting shadows, magic weaves.
In this grove where whispers flow,
Nature's peace begins to grow.

Starry Night Adventure

Under a canopy of twinkling lights,
Where stars paint the velvet night.
Adventure calls in whispers soft,
In the Starry Night, dreams aloft.
Moonlight casts a silver glow,
On paths where secrets often flow.
Fireflies flicker, dance and play,
Lighting up the hidden way.
Owls hoot from branches high,
Guardians of the midnight sky.
Rustling leaves and gentle breeze,
Whisper tales among the trees.
Foxes dart with silent grace,
In the quiet, moonlit space.
Rabbits hop and deer roam free,
In the Starry Night's mystery.
Shooting stars streak across,
Leaving trails of light and loss.

Constellations tell their tales,
Of ancient myths and cosmic sails.
In this realm of shadows deep,
Where dreams and whispers softly creep.
A journey waits, a quest to find,
In the Starry Night, heart and mind.

Sunshine Meadows

In Sunshine Meadows, where flowers bloom,
Underneath the golden noon.
Fields of daisies, petals white,
Glowing in the warm sunlight.
Butterflies in colors bright,
Fluttering with sheer delight.
Bees that buzz from bloom to bloom,
Gathering nectar, sweet perfume.
Bunnies hop in playful chase,
Through the meadow's gentle space.
Birds above in azure sky,
Singing melodies that fly.
Tall grass sways in gentle breeze,
Whispering secrets to the trees.
Ladybugs with spots of red,
Climb on leaves, their paths they tread.
Dragonflies with wings so clear,
Darting near the crystal clear.
Pond where frogs in chorus sing,
In Sunshine Meadows, joy takes wing.
Picnic blankets spread with care,
Laughter fills the sunny air.
Children play with hearts so light,
In this meadow, pure delight.

Whimsical Woodland Whispers

Deep within the heart of trees,
Where sunlight filters through the leaves.
Whimsical Woodland Whispers play,
In the forest, night and day.
Mossy paths and dappled light,
Create a world of pure delight.
Fairy rings with magic bound,
Where unseen creatures dance around.
Gentle brooks with waters clear,
Reflect the stars that twinkle near.
Toadstools red and mushrooms white,
Create a scene of pure delight.
Rabbits scamper, foxes sneak,

Through the woods, where secrets peek.
Owls that hoot and bats that glide,
In the woodland, where they hide.
Squirrels chatter in the trees,
Storing acorns, as they please.
Deer with antlers, proud and tall,
Graceful in the forest's thrall.

Tranquil Lakeside Serenity

Beside a lake where waters gleam,
Tranquil Lakeside Serenity's dream.
Reflections mirror sky so blue,
Clouds drift by in quiet view.
Willow trees with branches low,
Whisper secrets soft and slow.
Dragonflies with wings so bright,
Dance above in pure delight.
Fish that leap with silver flash,
Ripples spread where waters splash.
Turtles sunning on a log,
Beneath the misty morning fog.
Wildflowers bloom along the shore,
Painting colors, so much more.
Birds that sing their sweet refrain,
Echoes through the calm domain.
Picnic blankets laid out neat,

Feasting on a simple treat.
Gentle breeze and sunlit rays,
In Tranquil Lakeside's peaceful phase.
As twilight falls, stars appear,
Shining bright and crystal clear.
Whispers linger, night descends,
Tranquil Lakeside, journey ends.

Moonlit Grove Melodies

Beneath the canopy of ancient trees,
Where shadows dance in gentle breeze.
Moonlit Grove, serene and still,
Echoes with a magic thrill.
Leaves that rustle, whispers hush,
In the moonlight's silver blush.
Fireflies flicker, light their way,
Through the grove where dreams hold sway.
Owls with eyes so wise and bright,
Watch the world with keen delight.
Stars above in velvet sky,
Twinkle softly, passing by.
Crickets chirp in rhythmic beat,
A nighttime symphony so sweet.
Fawns that graze in moonlit glow,
Nestled in the grove below.
Mysteries in shadows deep,
Where ancient secrets softly sleep.
Fairy rings and hidden springs,
In Moonlit Grove, nature sings.

Whispering Willow Waters

By the banks where willows weep,
Whispering Willow Waters keep.
Rippling streams, reflections clear,
Whisper secrets to the ear.
Willow branches, long and green,
Draping over waters serene.
Leaves that rustle, softly sigh,
Underneath the azure sky.
Dragonflies with wings so bright,
Darting in the dappled light.
Fish that dart in playful chase,
Through the currents' gentle grace.
Wildflowers bloom along the shore,
Colors vibrant, dreams galore.
Butterflies with patterns bold,
Fluttering in hues of gold.
Sunlight filters through the trees,

Casting shadows, whispers tease.
Mossy stones where waters flow,
In Whispering Willow's glow.
As the day begins to fade,
Sunset paints the sky in shade.
Stars emerge in twinkling light,
Guiding dreams through peaceful night.

Meteor's Wish

A shooting star streaks across the night,
A meteor blazing with fiery might.
Leaving a trail of sparkling light,
In the canvas of darkness, a swift flight.
Silent wish upon its tail,
Whispers carried by the gale.
Children gaze with eyes so wide,
Dreams unleashed, nowhere to hide.
Fleeting moment, a cosmic dance,
Across the sky in a swift advance.
Granting wishes, one by one,
Underneath the moonlit sun.
Oh, meteor, grant a wish tonight,
In your fleeting, fiery flight.
A secret whispered, a heart's desire,
Into the heavens, rising higher.
Across the universe you roam,
In the night's celestial dome.
Granting hopes, with every glance,
In a meteor's wishful trance.
So make a wish as you gaze above,
With stars and meteors filled with love.
In the meteor's brief delight,
Dreams take flight, in the silent night.

Eclipse's Embrace

In the dance of sun and moon, they meet,
A celestial waltz, so grand and sweet.
Sunlight dims, shadows interlace,
In the moonlit glow, Eclipse's embrace.
Day turns to twilight, a mystical veil,
Moon's shadow cast, a cosmic tale.
Darkness falls in a gentle sweep,
As the world below is held in sleep.
Birds roost quietly, creatures pause,
In the eclipse's silent applause.
Stars peek out in the dusky sky,
In the embrace of night, they lie.
A moment frozen, time stands still,
In the eclipse's tranquil thrill.
Sun and moon, a cosmic sight,
In the heavens' graceful flight.
Eclipse's embrace, a fleeting kiss,
Nature's wonder, we reminisce.
A union brief, yet so profound,

In the skies, where dreams are found.
So gaze above with awe and grace,
Witness the eclipse's embrace.
A celestial ballet, hand in hand,
In the cosmic dance, where dreams expand.

Milky Way's Maze

In the depths of cosmic night,
Where stars ignite with dazzling light.
A spiral swirl, a celestial blaze,
Navigating through the Milky Way's maze.
Billions of stars in glittering array,
Painting galaxies in astral ballet.
Nebulas bloom with colors bright,
In the vast expanse of cosmic flight.
Planets orbit in silent grace,
Around their suns, a stellar embrace.
Moons in orbit, companions true,
In the Milky Way's grand debut.
Black holes lurk with mysterious sight,
Gravity's pull in eternal night.
Interstellar dust and gas, a cosmic haze,
Shaping paths in Milky Way's maze.
A billion years of cosmic quest,
A tapestry woven at nature's behest.
A universe vast, beyond our gaze,
In the Milky Way's infinite maze.
So gaze upon the starlit sky,
Where galaxies twirl, and comets fly.
In the Milky Way's celestial blaze,
A cosmic journey, in awe and praise.

Friends Forever

Friends forever, hand in hand,
Together we will always stand.
Through sunny days and stormy weather,
We'll be friends now and forever.
Laughing loud and playing games,
Sharing secrets, never tame.
In the playground, side by side,
With our friendship, we have pride.
When you're sad, I'll be there too,
To cheer you up, it's what friends do.
Hugs and smiles, and high-fives too,
In our friendship, we stay true.
Building castles in the sand,
Imagining adventures grand.
Climbing trees and chasing dreams,
With friends, life's never what it seems.
So let's celebrate our bond so strong,

With laughter, joy, and friendship song.
Forever friends, you and me,
Together, happy as can be.

School Days

In the morning light, we start our day,
At school where friends come out to play.
Books and pencils, desks in rows,
Learning new things as knowledge grows.
Teachers greet us with a smile,
Guiding us through every mile.
Numbers, letters, shapes, and art,
Discovering the world, we'll start.
In the classroom, stories read,
Imagination, worlds we tread.
Science experiments, hands-on fun,
Exploring how things get done.
Recess time, a joyful break,
Running, jumping, games we make.
Swing on swings and climb up high,
Underneath the open sky.
Lunchtime brings us all together,
Sharing meals, in any weather.
Talking, laughing, stories share,
With our friends who really care.

Afternoon lessons, tasks to do,
Writing stories, solving clues.
Drawing pictures, colors bright,
In the classroom's gentle light.

Beach Day Fun

Down to the beach, we're on our way,
Excited for a sunny day.
With sandy shores and waves so blue,
There's so much fun for us to do.
Sandcastles rise, tall and grand,
Built with teamwork, hand in hand.
Shells and pebbles, treasures bright,
Gleam and sparkle in the light.
Splashing in the waves so high,
Laughing as they crash nearby.
Jumping over, diving through,
Feeling the ocean, cool and blue.
Seagulls soaring overhead,
Looking for some crumbs of bread.
Crabs that scuttle, side to side,
Digging holes where they can hide.
Under the shade of big beach hats,
We play and laugh and chat with friends.
Ice cream cones that quickly melt,
Cool us down, joyfully felt.

Collecting seashells, smooth and round,
Listening to their ocean sound.
Skipping stones on water's face,
Watching ripples find their place.

Sky High Journey

Up in the sky, so high and free,
An airplane flies, come look and see.
With wings so wide, it soars above,
Through clouds so fluffy, like a dove.
Fasten seatbelts, engines roar,
We're ready for adventure, so much more.
Windows show the world below,
Tiny cars and towns that glow.
Takeoff feels like a gentle push,
Rising up with a mighty whoosh.
Clouds like cotton, puffs of white,
We're gliding in the bright sunlight.
Above the mountains, over seas,
Flying high, we feel the breeze.
Passing cities, forests green,
From up above, what sights are seen!
Pilots in the cockpit steer,
With steady hands, they have no fear.
Buttons, levers, screens so bright,
Guiding us through day and night.
Snack time comes with treats so sweet,
As we enjoy our comfy seat.
Friendly flight crew all around,
Keeping us safe, safe and sound.

Viking Voyage

Across the sea in longboats swift,
Vikings sailed through waves that lift.
With helmets gleaming, shields so bright,
They journeyed far from morning light.
Brave and bold, their hearts were strong,
With swords and axes, they belonged.
To lands unknown, through storm and rain,
On Viking ships, their dreams were plain.
In forests deep, they built their homes,
With sturdy wood and ancient stones.
Fires crackled, stories told,
Of dragons, treasures, legends old.
Warrior chiefs with mighty roars,
Explorers of far distant shores.
In fjords so grand, their voices sing,
Of quests and sagas, tales of kings.
Children played with wooden swords,
Imagining great Viking lords.
Learning skills to one day lead,
In the Viking way, with courage and speed.
Festivals with feasts galore,
Laughter echoing from shore to shore.
Dancing round the fire's blaze,
In the Viking nights and starry gaze.

Family Love

A family is a special thing,
With love and joy they always bring.
Mom and Dad and siblings, too,
Grandparents and cousins, all in the crew.
Together we laugh, together we play,
Sharing moments every day.
From morning light to evening's end,
Family time is time we spend.
Mom's warm hugs and gentle care,
Dad's strong hands that lift and bear.
Brothers and sisters, fun and fight,
But always end with hugs so tight.
Grandma's cookies, fresh and sweet,
Grandpa's stories, such a treat.
Aunts and uncles, laughter shared,
In our hearts, we know they're there.
Picnics, outings, holidays,
Family joys in many ways.
Birthdays, parties, special treats,
Gathering 'round to share good eats.
Helping hands when times are tough,

Family love is strong enough.
Cheering on in all we do,
Proud of me and proud of you.

Shawarma Delight

Wrap it up in pita bread,
With tasty fillings neatly spread.
Shawarma's here, oh what a sight,
A treat that brings such pure delight.
Chicken, beef, or lamb so fine,
Grilled and seasoned, simply divine.
Fresh tomatoes, lettuce crisp,
Add some onions, give it a twist.
Creamy sauces, garlic's zest,
Makes each bite the very best.
Pickles, hummus, all inside,
A flavor journey, what a ride!
Rolling up, so snug and neat,
Ready now, it's time to eat.
Bite by bite, it's oh so good,
A favorite treat, as it should.
Lunch or dinner, any time,
Shawarma's taste is just sublime.
Sharing with friends, it's such fun,
Eating together, everyone.
Sitting at the table, all a-grin,
With shawarma, where to begin?
Crunch and savor every bite,
Enjoying shawarma's pure delight.

Pizza Party

Pizza's here, hot and round,
With a crust that's golden brown.
Cheese that melts in gooey strings,
Oh, what joy this pizza brings!
Tomato sauce spread all around,
Pepperoni, crispy, browned.
Mushrooms, peppers, olives too,
Toppings piled high for you.
Baked in ovens, nice and hot,
Every slice, the perfect spot.
Cut in triangles or squares,
Pizza's love is always there.
Pull a slice and watch it stretch,
Cheesy goodness, what a catch!
Bite by bite, it's such a treat,
Pizza's magic can't be beat.
Gather friends and family near,
Pizza night is full of cheer.
Sharing slices, laughter, fun,
Eating pizza, everyone!
Veggie, meat, or plain delight,
Every pizza's just right.

Thin crust, thick, or stuffed with cheese,
Any way, it's sure to please.

Fizzy Fanta Fun

Fizzy bubbles, orange delight,
Fanta's here, bubbly and bright.
Open the can with a cheerful fizz,
A sip of happiness, that's what it is!
Golden soda, cool and sweet,
Perfect for a summer treat.
Pour it in a glass, watch it foam,
In every sip, you're right at home.
Picnic days and parties, too,
Fanta's there, just for you.
With friends around and laughter high,
Fanta fun, reaching to the sky.
Refreshing taste with citrus cheer,
Bringing smiles to all who're near.
Sunny days and playful nights,
Fanta's sparkle, pure delight.
Cans and bottles, take your pick,
Open one, enjoy it quick.
Chilled and cold, it's such a joy,
For every girl and every boy.

Gaming Galore

Turn it on, the screen lights up,
Grab the controller, fill your cup.
PlayStation's here, let's start the game,
Adventures waiting, never the same.
Racing cars at lightning speed,
Winning trophies is all we need.
Jumping high or sneaking low,
In magical worlds, off we go!
Battling dragons, saving the day,
Or kicking goals in a soccer play.
Puzzles, quests, and journeys far,
In PlayStation land, be a star!
With friends beside or solo play,
Hours of fun in a digital way.
Learning, laughing, skill and cheer,
PlayStation fun, year after year.
Characters we love and know,
Helping them through highs and low.
From cities grand to forests green,

So many wonders to be seen.
Pause for snacks, then back again,
Fighting villains, making friends.
Building worlds, or stories spin,
In every game, we always win.

Elsa's Frozen Magic

In a kingdom far away,
Where snowflakes dance and ice does sway.
Lives Queen Elsa, strong and bold,
With powers magical and stories told.
With a wave of her hand, snow will fall,
Icy towers, grand and tall.
Frozen lakes and sparkling trees,
Elsa's magic on the breeze.
Her sister Anna, by her side,
Together through adventures wide.
Facing dangers, finding friends,
In a journey that never ends.
Elsa's heart is pure and kind,
Strength and courage intertwined.
Though her powers caused some fright,
She learned to use them, shining bright.
Let it go, her famous song,
In the hearts of kids, it's strong.
Singing loud, dreams taking flight,
In the glow of northern light.
With Olaf, Sven, and Kristoff, too,
They faced challenges and grew.
From Arendelle to icy peaks,
Their bond is what each heart seeks..

Soccer Stars

On the field, the players stand,
Football ready in their hand.
Whistle blows, the game's begun,
Kicking, passing, having fun.
Running fast and dodging quick,
Dribbling moves and clever tricks.
Teamwork makes the dream come true,
Scoring goals, we cheer for you!
In the goal, the keeper waits,
Blocking shots at rapid rates.
Defenders strong, they hold the line,
Midfielders passing, feeling fine.
Forwards sprint with all their might,
Towards the goal, a thrilling sight.
Crowd is cheering, loud and clear,
Every kick, we clap and cheer.
Coaches guide with plans so bright,
Training hard both day and night.
Learning skills and how to play,
Football fun in every way.
Practice makes us strong and swift,
In every game, our spirits lift.
Win or lose, we play with heart,
Every match, a brand-new start.

Cheesy Delight

Cheese, oh cheese, so tasty and bright,
In every bite, you bring delight.
Yellow, white, or even blue,
Cheese, we can't get enough of you!
Cheddar sharp or creamy Brie,
Mozzarella, stretchy and free.
Swiss with holes and Gouda sweet,
Every type is such a treat.
On a sandwich, in a wrap,
Melted in a cheesy trap.
Pizza topped with cheesy bliss,
Every bite, a tasty kiss.
String cheese fun, a snack so neat,
Cheese cubes make a perfect treat.
Cheese and crackers, pair just right,
A yummy snack from day to night.
Grilled cheese sandwich, golden brown,
Melty goodness all around.
Mac and cheese, a favorite dish,
Creamy, dreamy, pure delish.
In lasagna, on a plate,
Cheese makes every meal taste great.
Cheese in tacos, cheese on fries,
Cheesy goodness, no surprise.

Being the Best You

Being a good kid, oh what fun,
Starts each day with the rising sun.
A smile so bright, a heart so true,
There's so much good that you can do!
Be kind to friends and family too,
A gentle word, a helping shoe.
Sharing toys and games you play,
Brings joy to others every day.
Listening well in school each day,
Helps you learn and find your way.
Respect your teachers, do your best,
Hard work leads to great success.
Helping hands at home are grand,
Clean your room, lend a hand.
Little things that you can do,
Show your love and kindness too.
Speak the truth, be honest and fair,
Show everyone how much you care.
Apologize when you're in the wrong,
Forgive others, move along.

Use your manners, please and thanks,
Show respect, from kids to ranks.
Being polite in what you say,
Makes everyone's day bright and happy